HOPSCOTCH
TWISTY TALES

Rapunzel
and the
Prince of Pop

by Karyn Gorman
and Laura Ellen Anderson

W
FRANKLIN WATTS
LONDON•SYDNEY

This story is based on the traditional fairy tale,
Rapunzel, but with a new twist.
You can read the original story in
Hopscotch Fairy Tales. Can you make
up your own twist for the story?

First published in 2013 by
Franklin Watts
338 Euston Road
London
NW1 3BH

Franklin Watts Australia
Level 17/207 Kent Street
Sydney
NSW 2000

Text © Karyn Gorman 2013
Illustrations © Laura Ellen Anderson 2013

The rights of Karyn Gorman to be identified as the author
and Laura Ellen Anderson as the illustrator of this Work have been asserted
in accordance with the Copyright, Designs and Patents Act, 1988.

A CIP catalogue record for this book is available
from the British Library.

ISBN 978 1 4451 1630 3 (hbk)
ISBN 978 1 4451 1636 5 (pbk)

Series Editor: Melanie Palmer
Series Advisor: Catherine Glavina
Series Designer: Peter Scoulding

Printed in China

Franklin Watts is a division of
Hachette Children's Books,
an Hachette UK company
www.hachette.co.uk

To the dream team –
you know who you are!
K.G.

Once upon a time, in Far Away land,
the Prince of Pop was driving
through the forest when he heard
the most enchanting voice.

He was surprised to discover
that the voice belonged to a fair
maiden who lived in the highest
tower of a dark castle.

The Prince could not see a way to reach the girl until he saw an old, wretched witch approach.

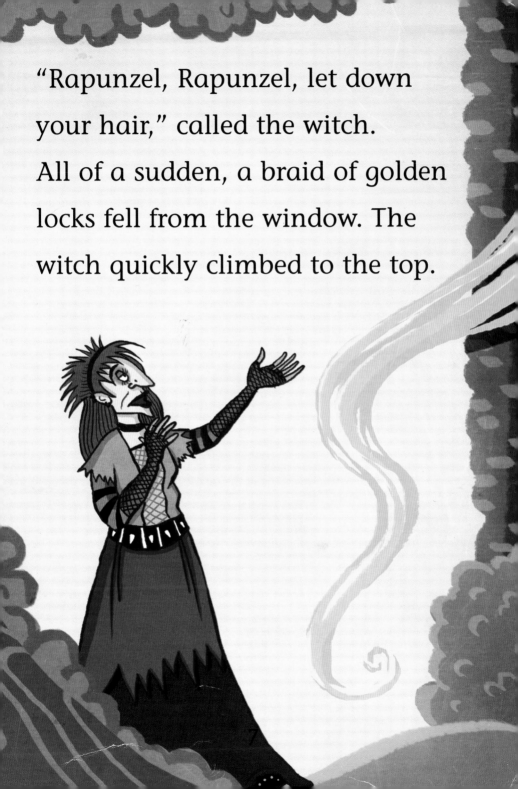

"Rapunzel, Rapunzel, let down your hair," called the witch. All of a sudden, a braid of golden locks fell from the window. The witch quickly climbed to the top.

That night the Prince approached the tower and said, "Rapunzel, Rapunzel, let down your hair."

Once again, the braid appeared
and the Prince began to climb up
until he reached the window.

"Who are you?"

Rapunzel screamed.

"I'm the Prince of Pop," replied the Prince. "I represent all of Far Away's top talent. I heard you sing and you shall be my next big star!"

Each night the Prince would visit Rapunzel in her tower to develop her act.

He coached her on her singing.

Instructed her on her dance.

And lectured her on
her "star appeal".

"You will make me millions," said the Prince. "But first we must free you from that awful witch."

14

Rapunzel looked doubtful, but she did want to be free.

The next night, the Prince returned
to free Rapunzel from the tower.
But when he called out for her,
she wasn't there.

17

In desperation, the Prince searched for his star all over town but she was nowhere to be found.

19

Then one day, as the Prince was passing by a recording studio, he tripped over something.

Far Out Fairy Tunes

21

The Prince followed the hair until he saw… "Rapunzel! I've been looking for you everywhere! Where have you been?" he screamed.

"I've been busy," said Rapunzel.
"I've been working on my
second album."

"But what about me?" spluttered the Prince. "What about my millions?"

"Sorry," shrugged Rapunzel.
"But I've decided to go with
another agent."

"But hey, thanks for helping me out," said Rapunzel.

The Prince was speechless.

And so, Rapunzel and her agent the witch lived happily ever after. And the Prince of Pop was left still searching for his next big star.

Put these pictures in the correct order.
Which event do you think is most important?
Now try writing the story in your own words!

Puzzle 2

1. I have star-spotting talent.

2. People can hear me sing far away.

3. I love speaking on the phone.

4. I am not really evil.

5. I want my freedom!

6. I love making lots of money.

Choose the correct speech bubbles for each character. Can you think of any others? Turn over to find the answers.

Answers

Puzzle 1

The correct order is: 1c, 2a, 3e, 4d, 5f, 6b

Puzzle 2

Rapunzel: 2, 5

The witch: 3, 4

Prince of Pop: 1, 6

Look out for more Hopscotch Twisty Tales and Fairy Tales:

TWISTY TALES

The Lovely Duckling
ISBN 978 1 4451 1627 3*
ISBN 978 1 4451 1633 4

Hansel and Gretel and the Green Witch
ISBN 978 1 4451 1628 0*
ISBN 978 1 4451 1634 1

The Emperor's New Kit
ISBN 978 1 4451 1629 7*
ISBN 978 1 4451 1635 8

Rapunzel and the Prince of Pop
ISBN 978 1 4451 1630 3*
ISBN 978 1 4451 1636 5

Dick Whittington Gets on his Bike
ISBN 978 1 4451 1631 0*
ISBN 978 1 4451 1637 2

The Pied Piper and the Wrong Song
ISBN 978 1 4451 1632 7*
ISBN 978 1 4451 1638 9

The Princess and the Frozen Peas
ISBN 978 1 4451 0675 5

Snow White Sees the Light
ISBN 978 1 4451 0676 2

The Elves and the Trendy Shoes
ISBN 978 1 4451 0678 6

The Three Frilly Goats Fluff
ISBN 978 1 4451 0677 9

Princess Frog
ISBN 978 1 4451 0679 3

Rumpled Stilton Skin
ISBN 978 1 4451 0680 9

Jack and the Bean Pie
ISBN 978 1 4451 0182 8

Brownilocks and the Three Bowls of Cornflakes
ISBN 978 1 4451 0183 5

Cinderella's Big Foot
ISBN 978 1 4451 0184 2

Little Bad Riding Hood
ISBN 978 1 4451 0185 9

Sleeping Beauty – 100 Years Later
ISBN 978 1 4451 0186 6

FAIRY TALES

The Three Little Pigs
ISBN 978 0 7496 7905 7

Little Red Riding Hood
ISBN 978 0 7496 7907 1

Goldilocks and the Three Bears
ISBN 978 0 7496 7903 3

Hansel and Gretel
ISBN 978 0 7496 7904 0

Rapunzel
ISBN 978 0 7496 7906 4

Rumpelstiltskin
ISBN 978 0 7496 7908 8

The Elves and the Shoemaker
ISBN 978 0 7496 8543 0

The Ugly Duckling
ISBN 978 0 7496 8544 7

Sleeping Beauty
ISBN 978 0 7496 8545 4

The Frog Prince
ISBN 978 0 7496 8546 1

The Princess and the Pea
ISBN 978 0 7496 8547 8

Dick Whittington
ISBN 978 0 7496 8548 5

Cinderella
ISBN 978 0 7496 7417 5

Snow White
ISBN 978 0 7496 7418 2

The Pied Piper of Hamelin
ISBN 978 0 7496 7419 9

Jack and the Beanstalk
ISBN 978 0 7496 7422 9

The Three Billy Goats Gruff
ISBN 978 0 7496 7420 5

The Emperor's New Clothes
ISBN 978 0 7496 7421 2